WE ARE A FOSTER FAMILY

How Two Young Boys Became Big Foster Brothers

Ashlee Carroll
Illustrated by Izzy Bean

Clovercroft Publishing

Published by Carpenter's Son Publishing, Franklin, Tennessee

Published in association with Larry Carpenter of Christian Book Services, LLC
www.christianbookservices.com

Cover and interior illustrations by Izzy Bean

Cover and interior design by Suzanne Lawing

Printed in the United States of America

978-1-952025-60-0

To my two most treasured blessings, Rhyder & Owen
thank you for teaching me to love more like Jesus.

Hi. My name is Rhyder and I am 6 years old! I want to tell you about how our family became a foster family.

My mom and dad told me they prayed about how to help others like Jesus did. Then they went to a meeting to learn more about something called foster care.

FOSTER CARE:

when parents can't keep their child(ren) safe, a judge asks other families to help love and care for them while the parents get better.

After my parents did a whole bunch of paperwork, they went to about one hundred classes to learn how to be foster parents.

One day, a man named Matt from our foster agency came to our house to see if we were ready to be a foster family. I showed him my favorite toys and he asked me if I was ready to be a foster brother. I said YES!

The next day, my parents said we were officially a foster family. My little brother Owen and I were so excited!

My mom said we could welcome a boy or girl and they could have dark or light hair, skin and eyes. Wow. I wondered whether I would get a brother or sister? Maybe both!

We talked about getting a baby or big kid – one, two or even three kids. Dad said that sometimes there are multiple children called sibling groups, and sometimes there is only a single child.

SIBLING GROUPS:

when two or more children who are siblings enter foster care, the judge tries to find one home for all of them so they don't have to be separated.

I know families come in many different colors and sizes because that's how God made them!

One night, my dad tucked me and my little brother into our beds. We slept all night and when I went into my parents' room the next morning, my mom was holding a baby!

I was so excited and a little confused. I ran up to her and she gave me a huge smile. I said, "MOM, is this our foster baby? Are we a foster family now?"

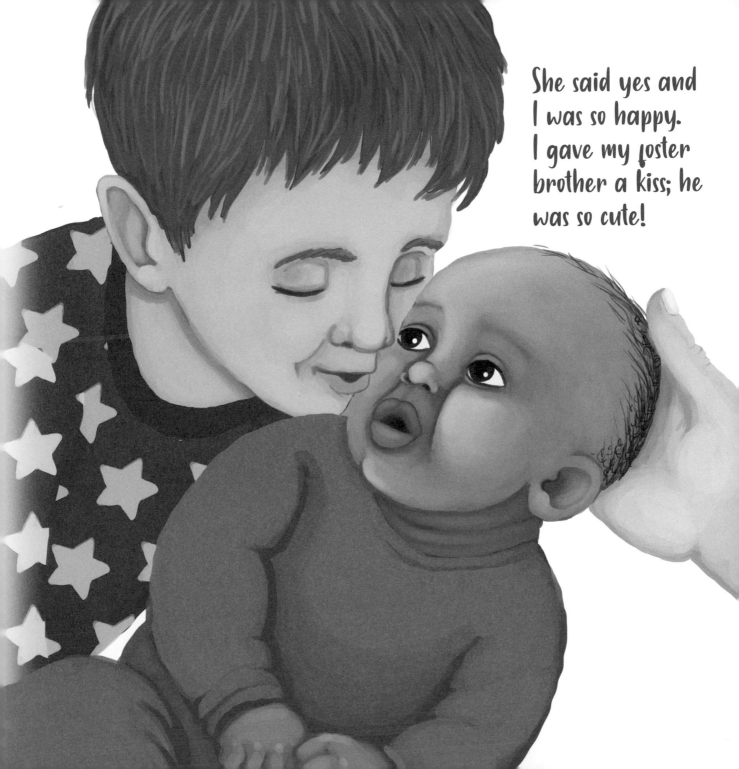

She said yes and I was so happy. I gave my foster brother a kiss; he was so cute!

Just then, my dad said, "Rhyder, last night, two children needed a safe home. So, we said yes and now you have one bonus brother and one bonus sister."

BONUS: the term our family uses to talk about brothers and sisters we have in foster care. It is important to use the correct terms, but we chose this to help protect their stories.

My mom and I hurried into the extra room we had setup and there was my foster sister! She was shy and just wanted my mom to hold her. I got a toy and brought it to her, but she wasn't ready to play yet.

SPACE:

to get ready for foster children, parents need to obtain a bed or crib and have space in a room for them. Sometimes, foster children can share a room.

The first few days were full of changes. Some were easy and some were hard. We played together, but sometimes, our new brother or sister would throw toys or cry loud. It hurt my ears!

Mom and dad had to hold them a lot and that made me sad and angry. Sharing toys and sharing my mom and dad were hard. Sometimes, I wanted my new brother and sister to leave so I didn't have to share anymore.

After a while, it was fun to have a bonus brother and sister to play with. I really liked helping them learn new things and how to follow the rules. At night, we would pray for their mom and dad to get better and thank Jesus for more days together.

One evening, mom and dad told us that our bonus brother and sister would be moving to their grandma's house. I was happy for them, but felt sad they would be leaving the next day.

I asked if we could see them again? My mom said that it was up to their family to decide.

The next day, my parents packed their stuff into the car. We all gave each other BIG hugs. My mom looked kinda sad, but she said she was happy that brother and sister would be with their family.

KINSHIP:

when a foster child or children are placed with an approved family member or close friend until their mom/dad can get better.

That night, our house was quiet. We had pizza and talked about our time with our bonus brother and sister. There were lots of happy times and some sad/hard times too.

Dad said that sometimes, when children go home, we won't see them again, but we can always love and pray for them. We talked about seeing brother and sister again in a few weeks. I was excited to go to the splash pad with them!

Then it starts all over again waiting to meet another brother/sister and become a foster family again! I wonder who will come next?